US MEN'S PROFESSIONAL SOCCER

BY JON MARTHALER

SUPER SOCCER

SportsZone

An Imprint of Abdo Publishing
abdobooks.com

abdobooks.com

Printed in the United States of America, North Mankato, Minnesota
092018
012019

Cover Photos: Julian Avram/Icon Sportswire/AP Images, (foreground); Shutterstock Images, (ball)
Interior Photos: Matt McNulty/Cal Sport Media/AP Images, 5; Brandon Parry/ZUMA Wire/Cal Sport Media/AP Images, 7; Matthew Ashton/Getty Images Sport/Getty Images, 8; J. A. Hampton/Topical Press Agency/Hulton Archive/Getty Images, 11; Peter Robinson/EMPICS/PA Images/Getty Images, 13; Richard Drew/AP Images, 15; AP Images, 17; Ron Frehm/AP Images, 18; Stephen Dunn/Getty Images Sport Classic/Getty Images, 21; George Tiedemann/Sports Illustrated/Getty Images, 23; Tom Pidgeon/Getty Images Sport/Getty Images, 24; Jack Dempsey/AP Images, 26; Vaughn Ridley/Getty Images Sport/Getty Images, 29

Editor: Bradley Cole
Series Designer: Laura Polzin

Library of Congress Control Number: 2018949103

Publisher's Cataloging-in-Publication Data

Names: Marthaler, Jon, author.
Title: US men's professional soccer / by Jon Marthaler.
Description: Minneapolis, Minnesota : Abdo Publishing, 2019 | Series: Super soccer | Includes online resources and index.
Identifiers: ISBN 9781532117459 (lib. bdg.) | ISBN 9781641856270 (pbk) | ISBN 9781532170317 (ebook)
Subjects: LCSH: North American Soccer League--Juvenile literature. | Soccer--United States--Juvenile literature. | Soccer players--Juvenile literature.
Classification: DDC 796.3346--dc23

TABLE OF CONTENTS

CHAPTER 1

ZLATAN TAKES OVER EL TRÁFICO

Zlatan Ibrahimović arrived in the United States just two days before the big match. At 36 years old, everyone called him just "Zlatan." Born in Sweden, he had grown up playing all over Europe. Everywhere he went, he won league championships. He won two in the Netherlands, five in Italy, one in Spain, and four in France. He had been injured for most of 2017. In 2018 he was healthy and playing for the Los Angeles Galaxy in Major League Soccer (MLS).

The Galaxy was playing its new rival from the other side of town, Los Angeles Football Club (LAFC). LAFC was a new team, but it was already 2–0 heading into its first game against the Galaxy. The fans of each team wanted to get a leg up on the other. They'd come up with a nickname for the

Zlatan Ibrahimović played all over Europe, including for Manchester United.

CHEVROLET

game too. Los Angeles is known for its horrible traffic. And in Spanish-speaking countries, "El Clásico," which means "The Classic," is the name of a game between big rivals. So the LAFC and Galaxy fans started calling their game "El Tráfico."

When the game started, Zlatan was on the bench. He had been in town for only two days and hadn't practiced much with his new team. Coach Sigi Schmid decided he should sit out at least to start.

The Galaxy fell behind immediately. Carlos Vela scored for LAFC just five minutes into the match. Twenty minutes later, he scored again. Early in the second half, the Galaxy scored an own goal. Suddenly Zlatan's new team was losing 3–0 to its new rivals.

In the 60th minute, Galaxy midfielder Servando Carrasco picked up a turnover and passed it to Sebastian Lletget. Lletget beat the goalkeeper with a shot. That made it 3–1. With 19 minutes left, Schmid decided it was time to sub Zlatan into the game. Almost right away, the Galaxy scored another goal to cut LAFC's lead to 3–2. Then Zlatan really got going.

Zlatan went from sub to star just minutes after being put in the game.

The ball got loose and bounced to Zlatan in midfield. Even though he was 40 yards (37 m) from the goal, he saw keeper Tyler Miller standing too far out of his net. So Zlatan launched a rocket of a shot. It flew over Miller and into the net to tie the game. The crowd and TV announcers went crazy. He had just subbed into the game in his first MLS appearance and already he was a star in his new league.

Zlatan leads his teammates across the field in celebration of another goal against LAFC.

The score was tied near the end of the game. The clock ticked past 90 minutes and into stoppage time. One of Zlatan's teammates got the ball and crossed it in front of the net. Zlatan was surrounded by two defenders and the goalkeeper, but he got to the ball first and headed it into the goal. After just 20 minutes playing in the United States, Zlatan had already scored twice. He had the game-tying goal and the game-winning goal. The match kicked off an intense and promising rivalry between the two Los Angeles–based teams.

Zlatan is one of a long line of world-famous players who have played professional soccer in the United States. England's David Beckham once starred for the Galaxy. French striker Thierry Henry played for the New York Red Bulls. And in the 1970s, George Best and Pelé played soccer in the United States.

American stars have helped carry professional soccer in the United States too. Players such as Landon Donovan and Clint Dempsey became famous around the world for their time with English club teams and on the US Men's National Team (USMNT). Then they brought their fame back home when they began playing for American professional teams.

Professional soccer in the United States goes all the way back to the 1890s. But it wasn't until the 1920s that a league gained popularity with Americans. Leagues came and went as pro soccer struggled to survive in the United States. But thanks to Zlatan and the many stars who came before him, MLS has gained a solid foothold in the crowded American sports scene.

CHAPTER 2

THE EARLY DAYS AND THE ASL

Baseball was the most popular pro sport in the United States in the 1920s. Other pro sports that are popular today had not really gotten started yet. The National Basketball Association didn't exist. The National Football League and National Hockey League were just beginning. And soccer wasn't even on the radar of most US sports fans.

The most popular soccer league in the 1920s in the United States was called the American Soccer League (ASL). It had teams in New York, Massachusetts, and Pennsylvania. Businesses ran most of the teams. Owners paid players to play soccer and gave them jobs in their shops and factories. The best teams were the Fall River Marksmen and Bethlehem Steel FC. They even recruited players from Scotland and England.

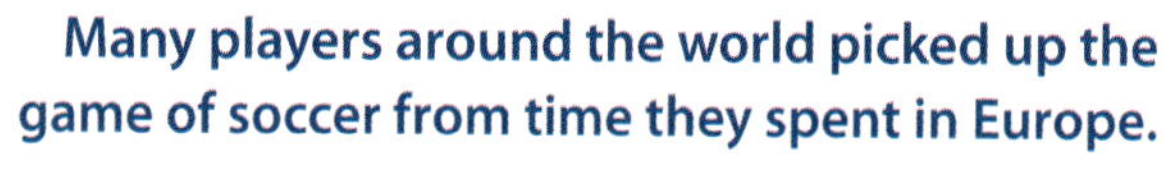

Many players around the world picked up the game of soccer from time they spent in Europe.

The ASL soon got into an argument with the US Football Association (USFA). The USFA was in charge of all soccer in the United States. The fight was about whether ASL teams could play in the USFA's tournament. The ASL did not want its teams to play a tournament outside of the league. However, some of the teams played, so the ASL suspended them. The USFA started the Eastern Soccer League for those teams. Eventually the ASL and USFA stopped fighting, but both sides lost fans.

When the ASL stopped playing in 1933, the United States was experiencing bad economic times. Most of the leagues that were left played local games. There were still amateur leagues in Chicago, St. Louis, and New York.

By 1960 sports were a big hit on TV. So businessman Bill Cox decided to start a soccer league. He called it the International Soccer League (ISL). Top teams from around the world such as Bayern Munich and Red Star Belgrade spent their summers playing in the United States. The league lasted for six years.

The 1966 World Cup was very popular in the United States. Ten million people watched the final. The next year, two more professional leagues started in the United States. The United

Teams such as the Wolverhampton Wanderers played matches in US professional leagues in the 1960s.

Soccer Association (USA) followed the same plan as the ISL. It convinced teams from around the world to come and play for the summer. England's Wolverhampton Wanderers won the league title playing as the "Los Angeles Wolves" in the USA.

The other league was National Professional Soccer League. Its rosters consisted of both American players and international players. At the end of the 1967 season, the rival leagues merged to form the North American Soccer League (NASL). It was the start of the first major soccer league in US history.

CHAPTER 3

NORTH AMERICAN SOCCER LEAGUE

The first North American Soccer League (NASL) season did not go quite as planned. Each of the 17 teams lost money. After the season, 12 teams folded. In 1969, to give the league more time to raise funds, five European clubs represented the five remaining NASL teams in a tournament known as the International Cup. That allowed the NASL to raise enough money to stay afloat. Its five teams played a 16-game season.

The league kept going by adding many more teams. Cities all over the United States and Canada received teams. Some of the teams lasted only a year. It was hard for fans to keep track of which teams still existed and which had folded.

The most important team was the New York Cosmos. Like the rest of the NASL teams, they struggled to get fans to come

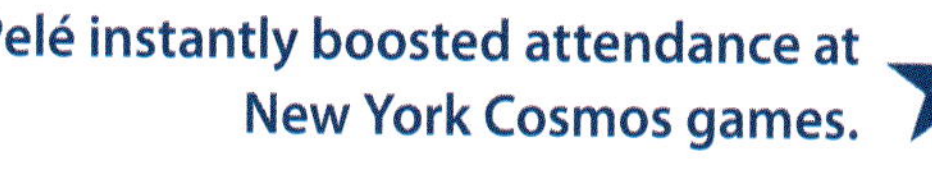

Pelé instantly boosted attendance at New York Cosmos games.

to the games. So their owners decided to try to convince Pelé, the best player in soccer history, to come out of retirement to play in New York. Pelé was from Brazil. He was so important to the country that its government had passed a law naming him a national treasure. That law also meant that Pelé was not allowed to play soccer anywhere else. The Cosmos needed permission from Brazil to let Pelé play in New York. It took a lot of work to make it happen. US Secretary of State Henry Kissinger even got involved in the negotiations.

It turned out to be a true game-changer for the NASL. With Pelé on the field, the Cosmos suddenly started filling huge stadiums with fans who wanted to see him. Wherever Pelé went, people turned out to watch him play.

Pelé wasn't the only big star to play in the NASL. German legend Franz Beckenbauer played in the NASL. So did Dutch star Johan Cruyff and Portuguese star Eusébio. British legends Geoff Hurst, Bobby Moore, and George Best also played in the league. These players were all at the end of their careers, but they were still big stars. Many new NASL fans already knew their names. They gave Americans a reason to watch NASL games.

Fans sat on the walls and crowded the bleachers of Boston University's Nickerson Field to watch Pelé (10) and the New York Cosmos versus the Boston Minutemen.

It wasn't just the Cosmos who became popular. The Tampa Bay Rowdies and the Seattle Sounders also drew big crowds. It seemed like soccer had arrived as the next big sport in the United States.

Pelé stayed from 1975 to 1977. In his last season, the Cosmos won the NASL title. The league had renamed its championship match the Soccer Bowl, a nod to the popularity of the NFL's Super Bowl.

Mike Connell of the Tampa Bay Rowdies, *left*, goes toe to toe with Rick Davis of the Cosmos during one of the NASL's popular indoor matches.

It was the first of four championships in six years for New York. The Cosmos also had the best regular-season record in the league every year between 1978 and 1983. With the most fans and the most money to sign players, it was hard for other teams to keep up.

The NASL also started an indoor soccer league in the winter. This version of soccer was played in ice hockey rinks on artificial turf. Each time had five players instead of eleven. It was so popular that another league, the Major Indoor Soccer League, started in 1978. In soccer the final score would often be 1–0, and there might be only a few shots on goal every game. Indoor soccer games often ended with scores like 10–8, and each team often had 50 or more shots on goal.

SI TAKES NOTE

In 1973 *Sports Illustrated* put Philadelphia goalkeeper Bob Rigby on its cover. He was the first soccer player ever to appear on the cover of the world's most famous sports magazine.

The NASL struggled to find American and Canadian players to play with the foreign stars. The league added rules requiring a certain number of North Americans on each roster and specifying how many had to be in the starting lineup. Despite this, the NASL never developed a star player who was from the United States.

In 1980 the league ran into financial problems. The country was going through more bad economic times. Teams started folding because they were losing money. The same old international stars weren't enough to draw fans. After the 1984 season, the NASL closed its doors for good.

CHAPTER 4

THE REBIRTH OF PRO SOCCER

The United States went several years without a professional soccer league. In 1988 Fédération Internationale de Football (FIFA), which governs soccer across the world, tried to jump-start soccer in the United States. FIFA awarded the 1994 World Cup to the United States. The biggest event in the world of soccer was coming to big US cities such as Los Angeles, Chicago, Dallas, and Washington, DC. One of the conditions of being allowed to host the World Cup was that the United States would have to start another top-level pro soccer league.

By 1994 some people doubted that the World Cup would be a success in the United States. It had been 10 years since the NASL had folded. Nobody knew if the United States still had

United States teammates celebrate after beating Colombia in the 1994 World Cup.

adidas

any soccer fans. But huge crowds attended almost all of the games. The tournament set the record for the highest average attendance for a World Cup.

The success of the World Cup showed that a new soccer league could be successful. Three new leagues were proposed. The United States Soccer Federation, which was in charge of soccer in the United States, decided there should be only one league. This would help the league because it would not have to fight against other rival leagues. It chose a new start-up league called Major League Soccer (MLS).

Major League Soccer found several people to invest in the new league. It decided that all of the teams would be owned by the league. This would prevent one of the problems that had tripped up the NASL. Owners would no longer be constantly moving and folding their teams. The league would manage things more efficiently.

The league finally kicked off in 1996. The first game was between DC United and the San Jose Clash. League officials hoped for the best. Many Americans thought soccer was a

Eric Wynalda (11) of the San Jose Clash fights off a DC United player during the first-ever MLS match in 1996.

Teams such as the Columbus Crew struggled to fill stadiums as the MLS fan base shrank.

boring sport because it can be very low-scoring. The league didn't want its first game to end in a scoreless tie.

However, through 87 minutes it was still 0–0. Then San Jose forward Eric Wynalda got the ball. Wynalda had been a star for the US national team at the 1994 World Cup. He had scored a goal against Switzerland. Against DC United, he performed a move called a nutmeg by nudging the ball through a defender's legs. He picked the ball up on the other side of the defender and blasted the ball into the bottom corner of the net for the game's only goal.

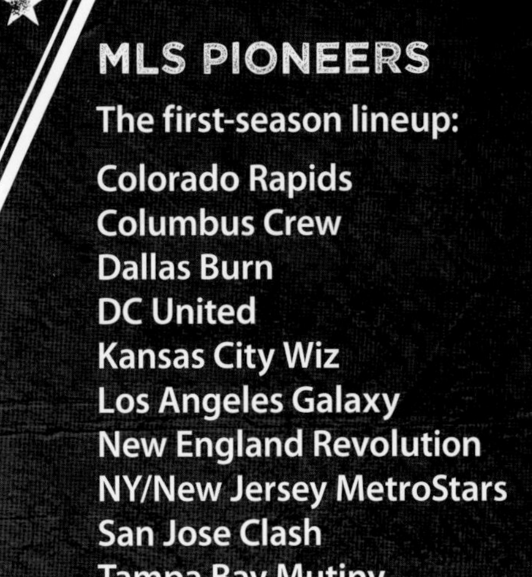

MLS PIONEERS

The first-season lineup:

Colorado Rapids
Columbus Crew
Dallas Burn
DC United
Kansas City Wiz
Los Angeles Galaxy
New England Revolution
NY/New Jersey MetroStars
San Jose Clash
Tampa Bay Mutiny

The league added two new teams in 1998. Chicago and Miami joined the original group of 10. Chicago won the league in its first season, the only MLS team ever to do so in its first year as a team.

Unfortunately for the new league, attendance was on the decline and the league was losing lots of money. It didn't help that most MLS teams played in huge football stadiums. The crowds seemed even smaller with all of the empty seats in the stadiums. Only the Columbus Crew played in a stadium that was built for soccer.

After the 2001 season, the teams in Miami and Tampa Bay folded. Unless something changed—and soon—it looked like MLS might suffer the same fate as the ASL, ISL, and NASL.

CHAPTER 5

MAJOR LEAGUE SOCCER TODAY

Just like in 1994, the World Cup saved pro soccer in the United States and Canada. In 1994 the US team had made it unexpectedly to the knockout round. In 2002 it did even better. It beat Portugal, one of the top teams in the world, and Mexico, its closest rival. The US team made it all the way to the quarterfinals. It lost to Germany 1–0, but many people thought the American squad was even better than Germany that day.

Fans wanted to see the new stars of the national team. Players such as Landon Donovan, Tim Howard, DaMarcus Beasley, and Brian McBride were now famous. Unlike the NASL, MLS had American stars for new United States fans to follow.

Soon more and more fans began buying tickets. Teams also started building their own stadiums. They no longer had to play

Landon Donovan was a huge star for MLS. 

21

in huge football stadiums in front of thousands of empty seats. The league started adding more teams again, but slowly. Some of the newer teams, such as the Seattle Sounders and Portland Timbers, even took the same names as old NASL teams.

Landon Donovan was MLS's biggest American star. His 145 career goals and 136 assists were more than anyone else in MLS history. The league named the trophy given to its most valuable player after Donovan when he retired in 2016.

In 2007 MLS also changed its salary cap rules, allowing teams to sign top players to bigger contracts. This made it easier to attract international stars to play in the United States. The first was world-famous English midfielder David Beckham, who joined Donovan with the Los Angeles Galaxy.

The Galaxy has been the best team in MLS history. Through 2017 it had won five MLS Cups and four Supporters' Shields, the award given to the team with the best regular-season record.

Other US professional leagues have also been successful. The United Soccer League (USL) is one minor league in the United States and Canada. It has been playing even longer than MLS. As of 2018, the league had more than 30 teams.

The Seattle Sounders went head to head against Toronto FC in the 2017 MLS Cup Final.

In 2018 MLS had more teams than ever before and was still growing. Its average attendance per game is better than that of the NBA or NHL. There is no longer any danger of the league ending up like the leagues that came before it. Teams such as Atlanta and Seattle average more than 40,000 fans per game. Almost all of the teams in the league play in their own stadiums. More and more players come from around the world to play in MLS. Professional soccer's journey in the United States has been long, but it is here to stay.

GLOSSARY

assist

A pass that leads directly to a goal.

cross

A pass delivered from the side of the field toward the middle.

folded

Went out of business.

knockout round

A round of a competition in which one loss eliminates a team.

midfielder

A player who stays mostly in the middle third of the field and links the defenders with the forwards.

own goal

A goal that is accidentally scored by a player against his own team.

stoppage time

Also known as added time, a number of minutes tacked onto the end of a half for stoppages that occurred during play from injuries, free kicks, and goals.

striker

A player whose primary responsibility is to create scoring chances and score goals.

Supporters' Shield

A trophy given to the team that has the best record during the regular season. A different trophy is given to the team that wins the playoff tournament at the end of the season.

turnover

When one team gives the ball accidentally to the other team.

World Cup

The biggest soccer event in the world, held once every four years. Players play for their national teams rather than their club teams.

MORE INFORMATION

BOOKS

Kortemeier, Todd. *Total Soccer.* Minneapolis, MN: Abdo Publishing, 2017.

Marquardt, Meg. *STEM in Soccer.* Minneapolis, MN: Abdo Publishing, 2018.

Marthaler, Jon. *Soccer Trivia.* Minneapolis, MN: Abdo Publishing, 2016.

ONLINE RESOURCES

To learn more about men's professional soccer in the United States, visit **abdobooklinks.com**. These links are routinely monitored and updated to provide the most current information available

INDEX

ABOUT THE AUTHOR

Jon Marthaler has been a freelance sportswriter for more than 15 years. He writes a weekly soccer column for the *Star Tribune* in Minneapolis, Minnesota. Jon lives in St. Paul, Minnesota, with his wife and their daughter.